MW01137973

TEARS OF THE WORLD

THE WORLD BURNS - BOOK 4

BOYD CRAVEN

TABLE OF CONTENTS

CHAPTER 1

Bobby stopped dead in his tracks, his body rigid.

"No," Lisa sobbed, forgetting what she was doing.

"Is he still alive?" Bobby stood.

"No," Patty said. "The man stabbed—"

"I mean the bastard who stabbed my brother!" Bobby screamed.

"Yes." Patty was sobbing now as she looked at Neal's body on the floor.

"Lady, please." Chris tugged at her, pulling her to the kitchen.

Bobby stormed out of the house in a rage. He had one thing in mind, one focus. He could hear shouts coming from behind him, but no one could follow. They were all busy, and he had to get ready.

He stormed into the barn and had just opened up the storm cellar door when he was met with a loaded rifle pointed at his face.

"What are you doing?"

"What's going on?" Melissa's father asked him, his hand steady.

"I don't have time for this." He swatted the muzzle away and pushed past the middle-aged man.

"What's going on?" Curt asked, concerned by the look of bloodlust in a young man he was starting to admire.

"They…they killed my brother…"

They talked for close to an hour. Bobby shed tears and made many vile threats as he paced the floor. All the while David sat on his bed, alone and ignored. He knew why they all hated him. If he was in their shoes or in the women's shoes, he'd hate him as well. He knew he was weak; he knew he should have done something rather than trying to just go along to survive. He felt ashamed. Worse, he felt like a slug, because despite everything he'd allowed to happen around him, these people let him live. Worse yet, they fed him. It was true he never had many friends in life, but they at least gave him some measure of respect by not killing him outright.

The problem was, he also had no trust. He did however, have an idea. One so bold and so outrageous that he thought it would work. He overheard Bobby relay everything to Curt, and he thought he knew how to accomplish a couple of really important things at once. Earn their trust, and show his sincerity. If it worked out, they'd have several problems off their back. If it didn't…they were dead meat anyways.

"Curt, Bobby," he said softly, trying to be a little louder than their hushed talking.

"Hold on," Curt said, waving at him dismissively.

Melissa, who had remained silent during everything, looked at David with tear-streaked eyes.

"Please, it's important," David pleaded.

"Not now," Bobby said, wiping at a string of snot coming out of his nose.

"I need to get to the radio. I have a plan."

"Shut up!" both of the men shouted. David winced.

The entire barracks fell silent, and everyone turned to stare at the four of them.

"I think…I…I think we can take out the rogue guard unit and Weston's murderer at the same time. Please….?"

The plea in David's voice cut through the pain that Bobby was feeling, and he slowly turned his head, wiping his nose again as he looked at the man they had captured from the raider's camp.

"If you're setting us up, I'll kill you myself," Bobby told him, his face going hard.

"Listen. I got nothing here. Nobody likes me, nobody trusts me. I know I should have done something before. I didn't. I'm not brave, not like you guys. I have an idea though. I hope you'll at least listen to me. I'm not asking you to trust me, not yet. I'm really sorry for what I allowed to happen and—"

Corinne suddenly sucker-punched him in the gut, and the wind left his lungs in a whooshing sound.

"Ok…ok. I deserved that," David said after catching his breath again. "But I'm being sincere. If you guys fall, I have no future. I'm trying to…I need…I want…"

Curt walked over and waved off the remainder of the squad who had started surrounding David.

"What's your plan?" Curt asked.

"We have to lure them together. Then blow them up," David said, his eyes showing the excitement in his voice.

"How are we going to do that?" Bobby asked. Despite his earlier dismissal of the former slaver, what the man said piqued his interest.

"Tell Gerard and the rest of the unit that I've located another target, and hopefully have them take out whoever it was who…I'm sorry about your brother. I should have said that first."

Bobby gave the slightest nod, acknowledging his apology. Then he waved his hand, motioning for David to go on.

"When we have them in one place, we can set off a charge of some sort."

"That's it?" Curt asked. "That's your plan?"

"They already know about the homestead because of the radio. I also told them you were all dead. Remember?" David asked.

TEARS OF THE WORLD

"Yeah?" Bobby said, confusion in his voice.

"Well, we blame your deaths on the guys who killed your brother. Maybe they raided this place. Makes the homestead a target not worth checking, and the other one golden."

Bobby was silent for a long moment, and he looked to Curt, who stood there with raised eyebrows.

"What do you think?" Bobby asked Curt.

"I don't know," Curt replied.

"Sounds too simple, doesn't it?" David asked.

"Maybe it is, but simple plans have seemed to work for us so far," Bobby mused.

They talked about it some more, and Curt was the one who supplied a key piece into a slowly forming plan.

"Blake is probably down for a while. He's shot up pretty bad. They think he's going to be ok, but it's going to take a bit," Bobby told them.

"Maybe it's time for those of us living here to earn our keep and show Blake how much we appreciate what he's done for us," Curt said, and a quiet murmur around the barracks picked up in volume as people spoke their agreement.

"I'm in," a young girl said, putting her hand on David's arm.

"If you double cross us to Gerard, I'll gut you alive. If you're sincere, then I'll owe you an apology. I'm in," Corinne said, her voice betraying her true feelings.

"I'm in."

7

"I'm in."

"Let's show the Jacksons they didn't make a mistake in saving us."

Different voices spoke up from the growing crowd of survivors.

§ § §

That night, Martha removed the bullet from Blake's shoulder, giving him a heavy shot of antibiotics and sewing shut his many wounds. Chris never left his side and even took his meals next to Blake. The next morning when Blake awoke, he was so stiff and sore that he had to bite his lip to keep from crying out in pain.

"Good, you're up," Sandra said, her eyes red.

"What's going on?" he asked, his head muddy and his senses confused.

"Martha knocked you out and took out the bullets and sewed you shut. You lost a lot of blood, and she used two bags of saline on you. It's all we had."

"Tell her thanks," Blake said.

"You can tell her yourself, once she wakes up. And be careful, Chris is sleeping by your leg."

Blake grunted and moved until he could see Chris's small form. The boy had fallen asleep sitting up next to the bed, and his small head lay against the mattress next to Blake's leg. Blake tussled the little man's hair, and he stirred a bit and then looked up.

"You're alive."

TEARS OF THE WORLD

"You got it, buddy," he told Chris.

"I was worried. That other man went to sleep forever."

"Oh no. The woman, what's her name…" Blake's mind couldn't make the connection. Her name floated on the tip of his tongue until Chris said it for him.

"Patty."

"Yeah, how is she doing?" he asked Sandra.

"She's been up half the night crying. Sounds like they finally…" Sandra let her voice trail off as she brushed tears away from her eyes.

"What?"

"The guy she was with. He finally told her he loved her right as he died," Sandra said softly.

"Oh no, that's rough," Blake said, trying not to choke up.

"It is."

"I smell food cooking," he said, changing the subject.

"I'll go get you some. Martha said you have to stay off your leg for a little while. She doesn't want you to tear out the stitches, and neither do I."

"My back is killing me," he grumbled.

"I'll go see if you can have something for the pain. I know you aren't supposed to have aspirin right now."

"How come?" He rubbed his hands across his eyes, trying to wipe the sleep away.

"Don't want to thin your blood out."

"You're going to be ok, aren't you?" Chris asked.

"I should be. I'll probably be up and throwing a ball with you in a week or so," he told Chris.

Sandra gave him a sorrowful look.

"Ok, maybe not a week, but I'll be good. I promise."

"Ok," he said, smiling for the first time that morning.

The three of them heard more rustling sounds in the kitchen, and Sandra motioned for Chris to follow her.

"Love you, hun," she whispered.

"Love you too," Blake said. And he meant it.

They found that Lisa was already awake and working in the kitchen. She was cooking scrambled eggs mixed with smoked pork as she turned and looked at them with bloodshot eyes.

"You ok?" Lisa asked Sandra.

"Yes," Sandra replied as she squeezed Chris's hand tightly. "Just tired. Blake's up."

"Should I get Martha?" Lisa asked, putting the spatula down.

"No, no. I know he's in pain, but I think he's hungry more than anything else."

"I know I am," Chris said, giving Sandra's hand another squeeze before running over to sit at the dining room table.

"Where is Martha?" Sandra asked.

"Downstairs in the boys' old room. She finally got Patty to sleep. Want to make coffee for us?"

The women, now mother and daughter, worked quickly side by side. Once the percolator was set on the stove, Sandra took over the cooking from an exhausted Lisa, who sat down across from Chris.

"So if you are married to Mr. Duncan, does that make you my grandma?" Chris piped up, breaking the silence.

Lisa looked to Sandra, who just gave her a tired smile and then motioned at Chris with her head.

"I guess so," she said after a moment, a smile touching the edges of her face.

"Good." He scrambled off his chair and into her lap, wrapping his arms around her. "Because grandmas are supposed to spoil us."

Despite the pain of her loss, Lisa's heart warmed at the unexpected emotions flooding her senses and squeezed the little man back, one hand running through his hair like she'd done countless times before with her own sons. The smile that threatened to overtake her features before now showed, and she smiled as tears ran down her cheeks—tears full of love and loss.

"Breakfast," Sandra said, putting two plates down. She returned to the stove and made another plate before taking it to Blake.

She returned and got a plate for herself and joined them, wiping her own eyes. Chris scrambled down and got into a chair of his own and they started to eat. Sandra had planned on eating with Blake, but one look at Lisa and she knew her mother-in-law needed her right now. Blake understood, and they ate in silence until three quick raps on the door jerked their attention away from their food.

Bobby walked in, flanked by David and Curt.

"Excuse me, Mrs. Jackson, is Blake or Patty around?"

Sandra saw the slaver, and a jolt of anger coursed through her body as she tried to comprehend the gall the man had. They had just lost a family member, and Patty the love of her life. They were still waiting to bury Neal, who'd been laid out and covered with a heavy canvas tarp.

"No," she said between tight lips.

"Well, uh, it's important. I need to know some things about yesterday. See, I have a plan—" David started stammering.

"No," Sandra said.

"It's about Gerard and the guys who—"

"What don't you understand?" Sandra stood, her hand reflexively feeling for the pistol she now kept on her side every waking moment.

Lisa wiped her eyes and took in the somber faces of her son and Curt. Curt wouldn't willingly be next to Bobby unless it was important, and everyone in the homestead knew about Bobby's interest in Melissa. If they were together in this, in whatever David was trying to do...

"Ok, please...just...let me know when. I think I found a way to—"

"Come in and be seated. I want to hear this," Blake said from the bedroom doorway, sweating from the pain and exertion of getting out of bed.

"Is it a way to pay back those guys who killed my son?" Lisa asked.

TEARS OF THE WORLD

"All that and then some," Curt said.

"Help me to the table," Blake instructed.

David told them the details of his idea, and after a while there were smiles all around. Duncan, Martha, and Patty joined them soon thereafter, and a plan was hatched.

"What about his daughter?" Blake asked Patty.

"I think he was just saying that to get me to... you know, be with him. I think he's got a screw loose. I doubt he's even got a daughter," Patty said, her skin pale and clammy.

"We'll need some blasting caps or dynamite," Duncan mused.

"I even know where to get some," Martha said with a grin, and everyone but Blake and Chris sprang into action.

"Give him this," Martha said to Chris. "Because he obviously isn't going to listen to me."

Chris looked at the cane, then at his father, who just shrugged.

"Where did that come from?" Blake asked.

"Probably from the barn. It's full of junk. We ought to clean it out someday."

Blake chuckled. He took the cane and sat down to have a cup of coffee, which Sandra had forgotten to bring him with breakfast. It wasn't warm anymore, but it was exactly what he needed.

CHAPTER 2

ALABAMA, PRE-EVENT

N ow, tell me again?" Michael's father asked.
"Yes, sir. I'm to go to Daniel's after mowing. But…I still can do my camping trip, can't I?"

"I don't know. You couldn't keep from mouthing off to the deputy. I don't think it's a good idea."

"Come on, Dad. I promise that won't happen again."

"Oh, I know it won't. You're seventeen now. You want your car back, your responsibilities back, you have to act your age."

"I will. But please, I've got this new fishing hole all mapped out, and the catfish there…"

With a chuckle, Michael's father's resolve broke. He gave his son a grin and then punched him affectionately on the shoulder.

TEARS OF THE WORLD

"Ok, for a couple days."

"Come on," Michael pleaded. "I want to try to find grandpa's old campsite."

"Hun, we have to go. If we get stuck in traffic, we'll never make the airport in time," Michael's mother's voice floated out.

"Coming hun," he called over his shoulder and turned to Michael. "Do you have your topo map handy?"

Michael's eyes widened, and he almost tripped over his feet as he turned to run for his bedroom. A moment later, he'd returned with a laminated topography map and immediately found the Talladega National Forest lands just outside their hometown in Choccolocco, Alabama.

"Take the Skyway Motorway north, then 503b until it ends by the Pinhoti Trail. Follow it north until you reach the end of the lake. Follow the creek until you reach here." His finger stopped at a point that Michael put his own finger over. The young man laughed when his father produced a black pen from his pocket and marked the spot.

"Thanks Dad."

"Don't thank me. You're still grounded from your car. You'll have to take your bike."

A pained look crossed Michael's face for a moment but was gone almost immediately. He could go, and his dad had finally given him his grandpa's fishing camp location, one he'd been looking for since he could go out into the woods on his own.

"I'll manage," he told his dad and then gave him

15

a hug.

"Don't forget your mom."

"I won't, Dad." He broke the embrace.

He hugged his parents goodbye and watched as they drove off. A short plane ride to Galveston, and then on to a cruise ship. They had two weeks' vacation planned, and he had the summer off. One more year of staying out of trouble and he'd be graduated, and hopefully enlisting. His parents hated the idea, but his grandpa told him a long time ago that he may have to follow his heart. His grandpa grew up a couple miles from their family home on an old farm. As a kid, his grandpa would pick cotton in the summertime for pocket money. Michael's grandpa had nine siblings, and the family grew mostly all of their own food to survive.

Fishing was both a hobby, religion, and a way to feed the family. There wasn't a regular grocery store when his grandpa was a kid, and what they couldn't grow or barter for, they hunted and fished. Fishing was one of Michael's passions, and if his parents would let him out more, he never would have gotten pulled over with the chief's daughter in the car. They were pulling out of the dead-end road where they'd just been necking and fooling around a bit when the flashers came on. He'd pulled over, but the cop recognized Beth right off and had started threatening to call first her dad, then Michael's. He lost his temper, and his parents had to be woken up to come get him and drive him home.

That'd been a week and a half ago. Now he was

itching to fish, and if he could find it, he'd stay at grandpa's cave campsite he'd been hearing about for years.

§ § §

His parents called him as they were leaving port in Galveston, making sure he was where he was supposed to be, and then they too were off for two weeks. He stayed with his buddy Daniel for the required day after he finished mowing the lawns he committed to. Then, as he was slipping out to go home, Daniel's father motioned for him to head to the garage.

"Your dad called," he told Michael, whose face started to fall.

"Yeah?"

"He said you are still grounded from the car, so to take the big pack frame he has in his closet. He figures if you are going to stay out for a week or more—"

"A week or more?" Michael interrupted, excitement in his face and eyes.

"Yeah. He figured you suffered enough, and that you ought to have some fun. You just have to stay away from Beth."

"So the chief put him up to this? My dad is bribing me?"

A pained expression tugged at Mr. Norton's features.

"He didn't come right out and say it, but I think

so. Look, you're seventeen, and she's almost sixteen. That's not a big age gap, but the chief can make it a big deal, you know? You don't need that kind of trouble, kid. You understand?"

Michael paused a long moment before answering. "Yeah, yeah I do."

"Good. Anyways, have fun and try to check in every other day or so. Take your phone."

"I will. I just wish Daniel was coming with me this time."

"I know. He's been wanting to, but that mission with the church...I really wish you would get more involved."

"Maybe someday," Michael said.

"Ok, well...I can see you're ready to head out. Be safe."

"Yes sir," he murmured. Michael gave a mock wave and hurried home, two doors down.

"Kids," Mr. Norton grumbled.

§ § §

Michael left that Friday, his pack heavy on his shoulders. He figured it would take him a solid three to four hours to get to the trail and another couple of hours to set up camp, if he had enough daylight left to find his grandpa's hideout. The idea of the camp had grown in his mind over the years, and he was expecting it to be something truly extravagant from the way it was lovingly described. His father claimed to have gone there a time or two, but he never had the enthusiasm for it the way grandpa did.

Michael stopped often, taking sips of water to help counter the killing heat of an Alabama summer. Once he got inside the national forest's boundaries, the shade cooled him immensely, and he had to stop again to put bug spray on every exposed surface of skin. When he reached the trail head, he stopped and pushed his bike along until things got too thick. He marked a tree off the trail with some orange marking tape, locked his bike to the trunk, and kept hiking.

The topo map showed that there were gradual hills here alongside the creek that fed into the lake to his left. He was looking for one of the stream inlets before he could...

"There it is," Michael said, smiling.

The creek was right where it should have been, but it was hard to see. It was only about ten feet across and looked to be a few feet deep. The mouth of it going into the lake was choked with lily pads. He started following it upstream and found a crossing point where he could see the bottom. Unlike a lot of the national park's rivers and streams, this spot must have been far enough back that it wasn't littered with the debris of humanity. The volunteers who kept the trail neat and clean had done a really good job. Michael crossed and immediately went back to the map to look for a visual reference so he could walk in a straight line to where his dad had marked the spot. He found a tree, half dead and burned from lightning, then took his readings from his compass. It was the right direction, so he headed inland.

Finding the cave was almost like falling into it. It was far enough off of the Pinhoti Trail that he worried he'd gone too far. He thought he was a good twenty-minute hike from it. He stopped to rest and took his pack off. He set it down next to a tree and leaned back into it, wiping sweat off his brow. The evening was cooling, but the Alabama summers could still be scorchers, even at night. He took a long pull from his water bottle, and a dark shape in his peripheral vision caught his attention. Slowly, he lowered the bottle and turned his head, worried something had snuck up on him.

He almost sat down in the opening of the cave. It was only about four feet in diameter, and he would have never realized it was there if he hadn't stopped where he did to rest. He dropped his water bottle, pushed his pack out of the way, and crawled halfway into it. The opening had a gentle down-ward slope that consisted of rotting vegetation that had slowly turned into limestone.

"I hope this is it," he mumbled to himself.

After a few feet in, he had to make a turn to the right. The opening widened out, and the ceiling was high enough for him to stand in.

"Oh shit. Grandpa, what is this place?"

Michael tried to take in the dark shapes in the back of the limestone cave. The curve in the tun-nel prevented light from coming further inside, and everything was cloaked in darkness. The sharp smell of dung was strong near the entrance, but had dissipated in the back. He walked slowly, his feet crunching on the rocky surface. He found himself at the back of what he thought was a twenty-by-twenty-foot cavern. On one end, the ceiling loomed six feet above him, and it angled up to almost nine feet on the other end. Michael's shins bumped into something. He almost tripped, but he put a hand out to stop himself. He found what felt like heavy canvas that was draped over something.

"I need some light."

Michael exited the cave and grabbed his pack. He carried it into the cavern, set it down, and dug around a moment until he found his flashlight underneath his ground sheet. When he clicked it on, the first thing he saw was that he'd walked through an old fire ring placed near the opening. He moved his pack so the old ashes wouldn't make a mess of it, and eventually he worked the light from the opening towards the back wall. Right away he noticed fissures in the sides and ceiling, one of which had a cable coming out of it. The cable lay across a canvas-covered shape. He shined the flashlight around and found two more. One looked like a bed, and when he pulled the canvas back, he found an old army cot.

He pulled another canvas off the tall blocky shape and found it to be an old chest, except this one had a flat top, not rounded like folks thought of the old pirate treasure chests to look like. The last one ended up being an old camp chair, much newer than the cot or chest. He pushed all the canvas out of the way and then opened the chest.

He found something long and narrow wrapped in oilcloth, and he pulled it out and set it on the chair. Three bulky black metal boxes were hidden underneath that, and along the edges were framed pictures, the glass old and dusty. For a moment, Michael looked up and around. He noticed some rusty finish nails banged into cracks in the limestone and hung a picture from one of them. With his sleeve, he wiped some of the dust off the glass. He wet his thumb and used that until he could see the faces in the pictures more clearly.

It was his grandpa and his platoon. They were sitting on a hill, and by the look of the guns, it was either in Korea or Vietnam, but Michael wasn't an expert. He looked down and took out three or four more pictures and hung them up, his heart racing with excitement. He searched around the chest some more and found an old leather-bound book that he had at first thought was part of the metal boxes. He blew the dust off of it and looked inside.

His grandfather's scrawl was familiar. Michael smiled and set the book on the oilcloth-wrapped package and moved one of the metal boxes out. It was heavier than it looked, but not terrible. He pulled all three out and found an old handset to talk into. It was a radio of some sort. A hand crank and several green ammo cans with the old Winchester emblem completed his findings. He thought he knew what was in the cans, and he was pretty sure he knew what was in the oilcloth.

Memories. This cave had been his grandfather's special place as a kid, and when he returned from war, half his adulthood gone, he'd been adrift for a while. This was his sanctuary. Wanting to conserve the batteries on his light, Michael took the oil-cloth package to the opening of the cave to find his grandfather's M2 carbine, the next in the evolution of the M1. It was a select fire .30 caliber carbine that had been tested over time. It had four of the boxy magazines, one of them especially short, the others longer than his hand. With a gulp, he wrapped them back up and returned them to the cave, putting them back in the chest.

The boxes and hand crank intrigued him as much as finding his grandfather's gun, but he was even more curious about the leather-bound journal. There were so many things that Michael had wanted to ask his grandfather, but death had taken him just after New Year's. He'd been sick for a while, and it was almost a relief when he died in his sleep free of pain. Now, maybe he could find out.

"And I came here to fish," he mumbled to himself.

He took the journal outside where he could read in the daylight, happy and proud at his findings and more than a little excited about the gun. His father had to have known. Other than lipping off to the deputy, he'd been a good, responsible kid, so his parents generally trusted him. That reminded him about checking in. He pulled out his cell phone to make the call when a flash of light almost blinded him. He struggled to stay standing, but he sat down, covering his eyes. Whatever it was, it was bright but far off. Almost as bad as looking directly into the sun.

A weird whistling sound had him looking up as his eyes were clearing, and what he saw terrified him. A passenger jet, miles and miles away, was falling out of the sky. He was sure of that fact, because the wings were tipping up and down and side to side, but the jet was losing altitude. He knew Atlanta was in that direction. When he lost sight of the jet in the tree line, the sound of the crash was a soft thump that he could feel. Other smaller thumps made him flinch over and over. Forgetting the cave, the journal, or anything else, he jogged for almost ten minutes until he found the stream and headed to the lake where he could see further.

Trailers of smoke rose in the distance, and the silence he'd taken for granted was deafening all of a sudden. One plane had crashed for sure, and if he believed and felt what his senses told him, many many more had as well over the minutes that followed. He knew something was off, something was really wrong. Every fire and rescue unit in the world should have had their horns blaring. Even way out here in the national forest he would have heard that. There was only silence.

He pulled out his cell phone and wiped the sweat off his brow and hit the button. Nothing; the smart phone didn't turn on. He held the power button down, positive he'd kept it fully charged. Still nothing. He pulled the back off the phone, pulled the battery, and reset it. The phone remained dead.

"Maybe I was wrong," Michael told himself.

With doubts and only rising columns of smoke as evidence, he convinced himself that he was just dehydrated. Maybe the jet was coming into the Mobile airport and they had a new pilot. Surly the jet wasn't crashing. He would have heard an emergency response. Things were normal, he was just nerved up from his findings. Sure, his phone was dead, but maybe he'd bonked it during his hike up, or while climbing into the cave somehow.

"And I have to do some fishing." He smiled. "I have to get some dinner anyways, then I can hike out tomorrow and let Daniel's dad know I'm all right."

He was already mentally planning his trip out, but first, he needed his supplies. The fish were already hitting the surface of the lake, picking bugs off. A big bass jumped, and that cinched it for him. Fishing first, phone call last.

CHAPTER 3

THE HOMESTEAD, KENTUCKY

Martha had checked off the map each and every farm she knew of in the area that might have what they wanted. Sandra and her squad left shortly after David had made the radio call. To say Gerard sounded happy with the news of hot women and a mountain of supplies would have been an understatement. David's voice had a new strength in it, one the homestead could hear, but that Gerard had missed. They would talk to him about it later, but their convoy was now moving. Slowly, but moving.

Gerard told him to expect a deuce and a half and several old pickup trucks, because the modern equipment didn't work, and they'd had a breakdown and didn't have the parts to make the repairs. This was good news as far as Sandra was concerned. She

TEARS OF THE WORLD

had been worried that they were coming in with APCs. It was still doable, but the armor would have nulled the effect of their surprise.

"Before we start preparing for this, I'd like you all to encourage my husband to sit down and rest. He won't listen to me," Sandra said to the group when they were on the land northwest of the barn.

"It isn't my place, he'd whip my—ouch Maw…" one of the boys they had rescued hollered up before his mom cuffed him in the ear.

Everyone smiled.

"At least sit," Martha said, and with a grimace, she sat down.

The mound of dirt was all that remained of the grave Neal had been placed in. They wanted to have Weston placed as well, but had yet to recover him. The plan was actually pretty simple. Fifty-five-gallon barrels would be filled with a mixture of ammonium nitrate and fuel oil almost half full. A scrap of wood would be placed on top of that, not so much as a cap, but as a float. Then heavy debris such as chains and even rocks would be placed.

Many of the roads traveled in Kentucky were carved right out of the hills. The plan was to bury the barrels into the hillside at an angle and time the charges to blow as the convoy came through. The barrels, topped with loosely capped lids painted to match the dirt that surrounded them, would essentially become a super-sized charge. The charge itself should be enough, but the old lengths of chain would turn it into something gruesome. Blake had no qualms about the homestead fighting dirty this way, and he prayed that they could find a solution that would keep them all safe.

There was only one snag in their plan: Patty had mentioned that the cannibal leader had a daughter. None of them ever saw her, and if she was innocent, she would need to be saved. If she wasn't... well, nobody wanted to put her down like a rabid dog, and nobody wanted to leave her for the rogue unit to have. It was something to be pondered later as they got more intelligence. Using Blake's directions, Sandra drove halfway and hiked the remainder of the way with two of her squad, Karen and Corinne. Neither of them were worried about what was coming. It was mostly a wait and watch duty, and as horribly as the cannibal leader was supposed to have been hurt, they weren't worried he'd get the drop on them.

They were to maintain radio silence and keep meticulous notes. With the two of them, one would rest, and the other would watch. For a while, it was both of them watching until Karen's eyes got heavy from the boring duty. Hour by hour, they traded off and waited for Sandra to pick them up.

Several of the men went out with Duncan, and they selected the points of ambush. It was where the road cut between a hillside and a sharp drop. The work was hard, but they eventually dug enough rock and soil loose to bury a drum before moving on. The angle would have to be perfect, so they left the holes to be filled in when the rest of the group found everything needed.

On o ne abandoned farm, they found almost everything they needed, including an upright fuel storage tank. Four of the barrels contained feed rations for the non-existent cattle, and one contained green pellets.

"Hey, do you guys want some rabbit stew?" Curt yelled. David and Bobby hurried out back to find several black-and-white rabbits hopping through one barn. They were munching on bales of hay that had been left on the floor. Several were drinking out of a puddle of water that had accumulated in a corner, where a broken board had let the rain in.

"Rabbit…hey, find us some cages!" David yelled excitedly.

"Why?"

"Don't dump out that last barrel. Its rabbit pellets," David told Bobby.

"Ok, ok. Curt, what do you think?"

"Won't take us long to catch them. Look." He held his hand down, and several of the adults hopped over and sniffed his hand.

"Why are they here? They should be in cages," David mumbled and looked around.

"Check this out, guys," one of the men they had rescued from the slavers said loudly. He was standing near two stalls that looked like they had housed horses at one point.

"What've you got?"

"Looks like they ran out of food and burrowed out," he told them.

"This was a colony setup," David said softly, opening the door and stepping over a short buffer of chicken wire that probably kept the rabbits from escaping when somebody entered their pen.

"So why did they stick around if they got loose?" Curt asked.

"They look pretty tame and…look, babies."

There were six men that had driven to check the farms out, and they had taken one of the trailers. Unfortunately it wasn't the one with the big cage on it, so they caught and loaded every rabbit and baby they could find into the bed of the pickup truck. David grabbed all the food and water dishes and dropped those in too. One full barrel and three empty ones were also loaded onto the trailer, along with ten bags of white crystal pellets. Lastly, a tool kit that Blake had left in the truck was used to un-bolt the upright fuel tank from its legs, and that was loaded and strapped down. If it'd been full, the six of them wouldn't have been able to lift it. As it was, they were able to move it enough to not crush their hands until it was in place.

"I hate to be the party pooper," Curt said, look-ing around, "but what are we going to keep the rab-bits in once we get back to the homestead?"

The sweaty men looked at each other and start-ed laughing. They stayed away from the house but checked a couple of the outbuildings by the barns and found an old chicken coop that had tumbled down. They took the metal feeder and waterers and went inside. Two large rolls of goat fencing lay to one side of the door with more T-posts than they had ever seen in one place. They hoped that Blake had a pounder for it somewhere, because none of them could find one. They loaded that mess between the barrels and the fuel tank before strapping it down.

"Where do we all sit?" Bobby asked.

The men who didn't fit in the truck sat on the edges of the trailer, and they kept the speed low and slow to not only cut down on the noise, but to keep the fuel from sloshing around. They had a vague plan of meeting up with Duncan's group near the lane to the homestead, and when they got there, the rest of Sandra's squad was there to watch the approach from both sides.

The ladies had hidden well, and anybody coming from either direction would be at an immediate disadvantage. Their spots had been chosen by Duncan before he'd left, and once he'd explained how and why he chose each spot, the ladies each identified a secondary fallback position. It wasn't difficult once they'd learned the basics. Now, they watched in disbelief as a little white nose poked up from the bed of the truck, followed by more and more.

"Are those rabbits?" a voice ghosted out of the brush, startling Bobby.

"Yeah, uh…"

Melissa ghosted out of the brush herself and rushed to the truck. She gave her father a look, then hugged Bobby before scooping her arms through the bed of the truck.

"Uh…somebody's coming," Curt said shortly.

His tone of voice made Melissa look up, and everyone tensed. There was nowhere to hide the truck and trailer quickly, so everyone took positions and got their guns ready as they listened to a truck coming down the road opposite from the direction they'd traveled. Everyone breathed out a sigh of relief when they recognized Blake's old Dodge D. Duncan was driving, and everyone looked relaxed and at ease. When they pulled to a stop, the trucks were pointing nose to nose about a hundred yards apart. Everyone relaxed as the men unloaded and headed to the one where Curt and Bobby sat.

"What the…" Duncan said as he watched Melissa smile and return to the bed of the truck, where she reached in and pulled out a rabbit.

"We'll explain later. We got everything you asked of us, except for the dynamite," Bobby said.

"I know where to get some. I'm worried that the group is going to have some forward observers blazing in here soon. Here's what we have to do…"

§ § §

"Do you have eyes on the target?" Gerard asked a sweating David.

"Not right now. I've been watching them for two days," he said before letting go of the talk button.

"What did you see?"

"Several men coming and going. A woman

hanging laundry outside on a line. A couple young ones. Could be boys or girls. The women and children looked scared or pissed. I don't know which."

"Defenses?"

"There's a burned-out truck near the house by the driveway. Don't know what that's about, but you can drive straight up. There are no physical obstructions."

"Why are you suddenly being so helpful? You usually are a quivering sack of shit? I'm curious."

David sighed and looked at the others. Bobby put his hand on his shoulder and gave it a squeeze. It wasn't meant to hurt or intimidate, but comfort. Over the past two days, David had really come out of his shell and surprised everyone. It was this confidence that Gerard had started to pick up on. Their eyes met.

"Just be yourself, to him," Bobby motioned to the radio.

"Gerard, I could have taken your gear and your coms and gotten away. Instead I'm helping you pick out a target."

"Yes, that's what I don't get." His voice sounded amused.

"Because I'm running out of food and I have no one to help me keep watch. With nowhere to go…" David let his voice trail off.

"So you think we'll just take you with us?"

"Well, I mean…I was hoping that…yeah," David stammered.

"Ahhhh, well, we'll see. I'm making no promises. I'm looking at a map here and there appears to be only two ways in before we get to the small interstate. How is it for stalled traffic?"

"Are you taking me with you when you go?" David demanded, an edge to his voice.

"How is the traffic?" Gerard said with a sniff.

"Dammit, I'm not playing games here. I want out." His voice cracked, and if he wasn't smiling, the homestead group would have believed that David was stressing out.

"Ok, fine. If you queer the deal I'll kill you myself. Got that?"

"I got it."

"Now," Gerard's voice was low and menacing, "how is traffic?"

"It's stalled pretty bad around mile marker one-ninety-eight, but opens up a bit."

"Enough for a small semi trailer to get through?" Gerard asked.

"Yeah. If you let me know when you are going to be rolling through, I can meet your men out there to help you push cars out of the way." As soon as he said it, he knew he was reaching, and Gerard's derisive snort was all the answer he needed.

"Well, I mean, I want to earn my place with your men."

There was silence on the line while they waited for Gerard to reply. Seconds turned into a minute. One minute turned into two. David wiped sweat off his brow and looked to the room of strangers staring at him, fighting down the panic of his public performance.

"You know, why not. I'll be rolling through there Thursday morning. Two days. I don't know the time, traffic's been a bitch."

"Ok. I'll meet you by the one-ninety-eight mile marker. I'll be on the northbound side."

"Two days, and there better be enough ladies there. You're sure on the numbers?"

"Yeah, one or two might be a little young, but that didn't matter to my cousin…" David spoke softly, his hands almost pulverizing the handset in nervousness.

"Not to us either, son. Not to us either. We'll pick you up after we hit the place. Gerard out."

David set the handset down and stood up, stretching. He noticed a quiet woman standing on the edge of the group. He'd heard of her, had known she was the one whose boyfriend was killed, along with Weston. Her red-rimmed eyes filled his vision as she came close to him and put her hands on his arms over his elbows. She looked him in the eyes then spoke.

"Thank you. I know I shouldn't want revenge and death for others, but I want Kenny gone. Dead, torn apart, planted deep."

"Thank you guys, for giving me a chance. I know you were all expecting me to double-cross you, but…I can't." He hugged Patty briefly before turning to face the rest of the group. "As bad as things were when you found me, you could have killed me. I know you kept me alive to talk to Ge-

BOYD CRAVEN

rard, but I've done that and I'm still here. Thank you for giving me a chance at redemption."

"Your performance was wonderful," Blake's voice rang out from behind the group.

Once again, he'd struggled out of bed and was leaning heavily on the cane Martha had scavenged from the barn. Chris helped hold his weight on the other side.

"Once this is done with, I want you to know something…" His voice was quiet, and everyone knew he was still weak from his ordeals at the hands of Kenny, Marv, and Jerry. "I've talked with everyone here in this room about you. We all can see how hard this is for you, how hard you are trying. A week ago I would have doubted your sincerity, but you just proved to me that when the chips are down…well…welcome to the family." Everyone smiled.

Blake thought the women and children would have been the first ones to object, but Curt's mother, the psychologist, had explained things to everyone in a way that made them open their minds and hearts. By her observations, David had only done what he had to do to stay alive in that camp. Not once did he ever do more than talk mean and tough to any of them. On several occasions, he had secretly snuck some of them food or a blanket, aspirin, or some other small comfort when nobody was watching. Once they all started sharing stories, they realized that David was one of the last vestiges of the horror and hatred they felt for their captivity and abuse. Once that was realized, they didn't have much to say. Curt's mother called it the beginning of their true healing.

Duncan was the one who had been somewhat of a hold-out, but his mind was changed the previous day when he was finishing the outdoor rabbit pen. The kids had been flocking the rabbit enclosure almost nonstop. Even though he'd helped mix and set the charges in the hillside and filled things back in, he still pounded posts and hung fences in the rich grass. He opened a makeshift gate that let the rabbits out of the small stall in the barn to the grass, and they took off like a shot. A little girl squeaked in delight, her hands clapping at the sight of two dozen rabbits and their weaned offspring running through the grass. David never hesitated. He picked her up and set her down inside the enclosure before jumping the fence himself.

Duncan almost started running, but Lisa had put a hand on his arm. Duncan hesitated and watched as another kid approached. David lifted that child over too. Soon, all of the little ones were inside, and David motioned for them to sit down. It wasn't five minutes before the children's laughter filled the summer evening as rabbits started hopping up to the kids. Some of the rabbits were scared, but most had been pretty tame to begin with.

"You know, he isn't a half-bad guy," Lisa had remarked, and that was the moment Duncan knew it was time for forgiveness.

Sandra had always doubted that David was as

evil as the others. He seemed like a quiet guy who got bullied into a situation, so when Blake spoke up to the group, she turned and hurried to his side to usher him into a chair.

"Come on now, really. You aren't supposed to be up," Sandra told him.

"I had something to say. It's your home too," he said aloud, not to his wife, but to the group. "We work together, we protect each other. If needed, we die together, but not after we do our best to send Gerard and his boys to hell first."

"What's in hell?" Chris's little voice cut through the cheers that had broken the silence. At the boy's question, the cheers turned into outright laughter.

"Just the bad guys, little man. Just the bad guys," Blake told him, running his hand through his adopted son's hair.

"Good, then let's send all the bad guys there."

This brought down the house, and when the group composed themselves again after what never would have been funny in any other time or place, they planned. If Gerard was telling the truth, the first forward observers would be through tonight or tomorrow. The ladies who had been watching Kenny's hunting lodge had been recalled, debriefed, and traded out for fresh bodies to watch the roadside for the FOs. Only two tics on the handset would be their signal that they had gone past, so somebody always sat by the radio. Since Blake had been laid up, that was going to be him.

"Those of you who can, get some rest. I want to

know if the FOs appear to be suspicious or onto us. The fact that there probably isn't a ton of women and children at the lodge will make them nervous enough. That's when we take them out. Let's let Gerard assume something bad happened or the hills are blocking the signal. Does everyone know what they are doing?" Sandra's voice was quick and precise.

"No," came the response that echoed all around the room.

"I wouldn't want to piss her off," Curt told Bobby in a hushed voice.

"No you don't. She'd tear your arm off and beat you with it," Bobby said with a deadpan expression on his face. The room suddenly went quiet.

He realized he'd just been overheard, and everyone was now looking at him. A flush crept up his cheeks, and he looked at Sandra, who had her arms around Blake.

"I was just telling Curt here about how I met you."

Blake laughed and Sandra snorted, and everyone smiled. Even Duncan was grinning ear to ear, and Lisa gave him a puzzled look.

"When he tried to uh…introduce himself to Sandra?" Blake told her. Lisa's expression changed and she chuckled.

"What?" Curt asked.

"She laid some kung fu on your son-in-law."

"My son-in-law…? Wait, is there something—"

Curt's question was cut off when Bobby ran out

the front door. A swearing and cussing Curt gave chase.

Everyone busted up again, and Blake told Sandra she better save Bobby from a father's wrath. He was innocent as far as everyone knew, as the barracks afforded little privacy.

CHAPTER 4

PINHOTI TRAIL, ALABAMA

Michael awoke. He was confused at first by the utter lack of illumination. He swung his legs off the end of the cot, feeling cold and stiff all over. He rubbed his arms to get the circulation going again and then pushed his sleeping bag off of his body as he stood up. He stretched, feeling his shoulders and back pop. The damp smell of the cave brought back memories of how he got there. He was still full from his meal the night before, but needed to take his camp shovel and go dig a hole somewhere.

He crawled out of the cave, and the smell of smoke was evident immediately. With no fire in sight, he decided to hike towards the lake again, hoping the break in the skyline would let him see. He grabbed his small daypack and headed out. After a while, Michael made it there. Instead of the small columns of smoke he had seen last night, they were towering, blooming and huge. Five thousand planes. The thought intruded into the forefront of his brain. Five thousand planes in the sky over the country at any given moment. He shivered. He had felt the impacts, at first feared they were planes, but then dismissed it.

"It couldn't have been," Michael said to no one.

He filled two water bottles with his small Katadyn filter and started to hike out towards his bike. The humidity wasn't bad, and the mosquitoes weren't requesting landing clearance, so the walk wasn't unpleasant. But in the pit of his stomach, he thought there was something off, something wrong. He knew it. Feeling the pangs of fear, the voice startled him after being alone on the Pinhoti for a while.

"Excuse me?" a man said, stepping out onto the trail just in front of Michael.

"Oh, uh, hi," Michael said, unsure what else to say.

The man was obviously a novice hiker or camping enthusiast. His shoes were brand new, and his clothing had the crisp lines of being recently starched. He would have blisters and a rash if he wasn't careful. He was pudgy, somewhere in his mid-forties if Michael had to guess. His face was sweaty, and his voice was high and thin despite the eighty pounds of size difference he had over Michael.

TEARS OF THE WORLD

"Hey, uh, can you help me break the chain on this?" the man motioned to Michael's bike.

"No…it's my bike."

"Oh hey, I need it. The car won't start, and my cell phone died sometime last night. I need to ride into town and make a call."

"My phone is dead too," Michael told him, shocked that this man was trying to steal his bike and seemed ok with it.

"Ok, so, unlock this and we'll be good. I'll bring it back with the tow truck."

Michael's bad feeling only got worse. The guy was going to be a pain, an insistent pain.

"No, it's my bike. I've got to ride back and find out what's happening."

"Hey, I've got kids to look out for," he argued.

"I am a kid," Michael almost shouted back angrily.

"Listen kid, I need this. I'll bring it back to you later on today. What don't you get about that?" The man stepped away from the bike and tried to tower over Michael.

It worked. Michael took a step back. It wasn't so much that he was intimidated by the man with the Mickey Mouse voice, more that he was surprised that a grown man was trying to steal his bike right in front of him, using intimidation and suggesting strong arm tactics.

"Dude, get out of my face. I'm going to take my bike and—" Michael's words cut off when he was knocked to the ground by a sucker punch.

BOYD CRAVEN

The punch to the gut knocked the wind out of him and left him gasping for air. His back hurt where he fell on his daypack, and something sharp was poking him in the lower back. He saw the man move back to where his bike was chained and play with the combination lock some more. Michael was shocked, and he rolled on the ground, trying to force oxygen back into his lungs.

"What's the combination, kid?" the man said, putting his hands under Michael's arms to pull him to his feet.

Michael almost had his wind back. He frantically ran his hands over the ground, and as he rose, he found a rock the size of a baseball. He threw it and hit the guy in the temple. The rock glanced off the side of the stranger's head, and Michael was free. He crawled to his feet to see the guy on one knee, his hand covering the side of his head. Michael shrugged out of his daypack and held it loosely in one hand, ready to drop it and run if the guy came after him.

His ribs hurt, and falling on the daypack gave him a sore spot that he worried might be a bad scrape or cut. He kept one wary eye on the now cussing figure and looked at his pack. He'd fallen onto his folding shovel and belatedly remembered he hadn't had a chance to go to the bathroom. The stranger made his way to his feet and glared at Michael, the side of his temple red with blood.

Did I do that? Michael thought, the adrenaline in his body making him feel sick and shaky.

44

TEARS OF THE WORLD

"I'm going to kill you for that." The man's voice dropped two octaves, sounding masculine for once.

Michael walked backwards, not wanting to take his eyes off the man. He'd already proven that he was quick with his hands, and in an all-out sprint, he was confident he could have outrun the man if he wasn't already hurt. His ribs and back both protested loudly. An incoherent shout was all the warning Michael had before the man charged. Michael felt for the folding shovel with his right hand and swung it when the man was within reach. It made a sickening, crunching sound against the man's skull, and with his forward momentum unchecked, he slammed into Michael at an angle.

The wind was knocked out of Michael a second time before he pushed the limp body away. He had never heard something so sickening as the sound the folded shovel made when it hit the stranger's head, and he didn't dare look at his face. He kept his eyes from the man's chin down and rolled him on his back.

"Please don't be dead, please don't be…" He felt for a pulse, like he was taught in all of his first aid courses.

There was no pulse, and with barely a moment's warning, Michael rolled off the side of the trail and vomited. He retched until his throat and stomach felt raw. His tears flowed freely. *I killed a man. I killed a man.* The thought played over and over in his head. The horror he felt was tremendous and crushing.

"I can't do it," he said between wiping his eyes and his nose.

He had to find help, had to call someone, do something. He pulled the body by the legs off the main part of the trail. He made no attempt to cover the body, as he hadn't planned on doing anything more than flagging down a cop as soon as he could. He worried half a second that he'd get in trouble, but the guy was acting irrationally. He attacked a minor. What he did was self-defense, wasn't it? He put the shovel back into his daypack, more out of habit than keeping the trail clean. Or to hide evidence. Michael pushed the thought aside and went to his bike. He had the combination open within a few turns, and wound the chain up under the seat and locked it back into place.

He got onto the bike and started towards the road that would take him back to civilization. His muscles were still shaky and he twitched from the adrenaline overload. The trail quickly led him to a gravel parking lot where one car was parked under a tree within walking distance to the public restrooms. Michael had a sinking feeling about whose car that was, and it was one more punch to the gut that he felt guilt over. He stopped his bike on the side and locked it once again.

He used the men's room, and out of habit, he turned on the faucet to wash his hands. Water came out, but the pressure wasn't great.

"Shhhh, did you hear that?" A young feminine voice startled him. There was nobody else in the men's room. He looked up and noticed the drop ceiling. It must be coming from the other bathroom.

"Linny, I'm scared. Where's Daddy?" The voice was different than the first, younger, no way to tell the gender.

"He went to go find help. Now you have to be quiet; you don't want wild animals to eat you. Shhhhhh."

"Uhhh, hello?" Michael called out, his voice echoing in the cinder block room.

"Daddy?" the little voice called hopefully.

Michael walked out of the open side doorway and around the corner. There was a drinking fountain near the women's restroom, and he stood there and waited until two kids walked out. A girl, no more than ten, was holding the hand of her younger brother, who had a crew cut. Both of them had a strong family resemblance to the man he'd killed in the forest. His heart threatened to give out when they looked at him in disappointment.

"You're not Daddy," the little boy pointed out.

"No. I'm sorry, I'm not. I'm Michael Lewiston," he told them, holding his hand out to shake.

"We're not supposed to talk to strangers," the girl interjected.

"Ok, well…I was just using the bathroom. Have you two been out here alone?"

"Yeah, for just a little while, I think. I slept some—" the boy started to say, but his sister squeezed his hand and gave him a glare to shut him up.

"Stranger," she reminded him.

"Oh, well, mister, if you see my daddy, can you tell him we're getting hungry?"

"I can do that," he said, fighting back tears.

"Here." He took off his pack. "I've got some granola and power bars." Michael pulled out all of his food.

"Well…" the girl began to say something, but the sight of the food stopped her.

Michael was having an internal struggle. He was horrified thinking about leaving them here alone, but he had to go check on things and call the police. He'd killed a man, very likely the father of these two kids. If the man had told him he had two kids to look out for here with him, it might have made a difference. Maybe he would have stayed down and never threw that rock…

The pile of food made the little girl look at him funny, but in the end, her stomach won her over. "I'm Linny, and this is Bret. Thanks for the food. You'll help us look for our dad? I mean, you're coming back, aren't you?"

"Yeah, I'm coming back."

"Good."

"Your car, it doesn't work?"

"No. Daddy said the battery died or something. My DS is dead too." The boy held up a square piece of technology, one that Michael himself owned.

"Wow, well…I'll tell you what. No matter what, I'll be back up here. It'll take me two or three hours

48

TEARS OF THE WORLD

to get home. Do you guys live around here?" he asked hopefully, wanting to leave but also hating to leave them.

"No, we're from New Hampshire. We're going to travel the Pinhoti and take lots of pictures," Linny said proudly.

"Where's your mom?" Michael asked.

"She died last year. Cancer," Bret told him, making him want to flee.

"I uh…I'll be back." He hurried to his bike, the tears starting to come down his cheeks.

"Ok, thank you," Linny called to him.

§ § §

His bike ride to Daniel's house was a lot shorter than he expected, but his sore ribs and shaky legs were complaining that he'd pushed himself, pushed hard. Daniel's father was in the driveway, packing an old three-wheeler with his lawn cart attached to it. Food and clothing were piled in the small trailer.

"Oh, thank God. I was going to try to come find you soon," John said, getting off the quad.

"What's going on?" Michael's chest was heaving still, sweat running rivers off his temples.

"I don't know, but it's bad. Nothing electronic seems to work, the cars don't work." They walked towards the garage and the shade. "And there were several planes that crashed."

"Five thousand," Michael mumbled.

"What's that?"

49

"Some random fact I learned in school. There are five thousand jets flying over America at any given moment. I wasn't imagining things, was I?" Michael's voice was bewildered.

Michael sat on the edge of the cracked pavement and took the bottle of water John offered before he sat next to him.

"I'm glad your parents were already landed then, they should be safe."

"What are you talking about?"

"Do you remember what I did before I was a plumber?"

"You were in the air force?"

"No, navy. I'm pretty sure we had an EMP or a CME go off. It fries circuit boards. If I'm right, things are about to get really, really bad."

"Are my parents going to be ok?"

"The ship they're on is going to be fine if they made it away from the coast. They should have been outside the effects. Now, I need you to pack your stuff and together we'll—"

"You're leaving for somewhere," he stated, not understanding the man's sudden urgency.

"Yes, we have to get you packed up," Mr. Norton said, walking to the three-wheeler.

"There's something I have to do first," Michael said, and with a fresh flow of tears, explained everything.

He'd never cried this hard in his entire life; it left him feeling crushed and hollow. When he was done explaining everything, John remained silent for a long moment.

"We can try to talk to the chief if you'd like. I don't know if they would be in any shape to help."

"What do you mean? They're the police, they handle things like this." Michael was worried.

"Everyone has been thrown back in time by a hundred years. Things are going to get ugly. There are only so many of the police, and they are having the same problems that the rest of us are dealing with. No cars, no phones, no radios…"

"Is this why you're leaving?" Michael asked quietly.

"No, it's the fires."

The smell of smoke was a lot stronger, and he realized that he'd been smelling it all day, just not the variations of intensity.

"Five thousand planes…" Michael's voice trailed off.

"Like five thousand bombs going off, all over the country."

"Mr. Norton, do you—"

"John, call me John. Let's go try the police first. Then we'll pack you up and head out. Deal?"

"Yes Mr—I mean, sure, John." His voice sounded less confident than he felt.

In truth, he felt wonderful for having somebody to share the burden with, of not being stuck alone.

CHAPTER 5

ROBERTSON'S RANCH, KENTUCKY

I keep telling you that you should eat," Kenny told the still form in the bed.

No reply.

"Come on, sweetie. Look, I got your medicine. Hopefully this dose will work?" Kenny held the syringe up to the still form covered in a sheet.

He pulled the sheet back and pulled his daughter's sleeve up. He guided the needle to her shoulder and had to work to get it in. He depressed the plunger. When he pulled the needle back out, the old insulin dribbled out of the dried flesh of his daughter.

"I'm sorry sweetie, I hope that didn't hurt too bad." He put the Band-Aid he'd had ready over the spot, keeping it from making a mess. He pulled the sheet back over her body and tucked her in.

TEARS OF THE WORLD

"If you want breakfast, let me know."

Emily had always been a vibrant young girl, but it was quickly found out that she was going to be insulin dependent her entire lifetime. When things ended, there was a horrifying week when Ken had scrambled and finally looted a pharmacy. The insulin had been warm to the touch, and he knew how badly it degraded its usefulness, but he'd kept giving it to her, praying for a miracle. She grew weaker and more tired. Listless. She would sleep for long stretches. He hadn't remembered her waking up in any recent time, but once in a while, some of her food was gone when he was out of the house. So she must be fine.

Marv and Jerry moved into the main house. The only solace Ken had was the hunt. The thrill. The screams as he pulled his knife through another human's gut. With his morning ritual of the medication done, he took the uneaten food from last night to the kitchen, then went to the bathroom to use the mirror. He stripped to his waist and washed up.

Whatever the cold man had thrown into his face really messed him up horribly. Acid, probably, though he didn't think he had any acid in there. The fumes from it had made him choke and gag. He still had a hard time breathing after the fact, and the wounds were open and sore on his chest and half his face. If it got infected he was done for, and he'd have no one to take care of his Emily. He could forgive the cold guy for messing him up; he was pretty sure he did, even though he put a .270 round

53

through his back as they were leaving.

That felt good, watching him twitch in pain, but his focus was brought back to the mirror, where he used warm soapy water and a clean-ish wash cloth to wipe the oozing, weeping ruin of his face. It horrified him and it probably horrified Emily. That's why she must be ignoring him. He freaked her out.

"Kids. Who understands them?"

When he was done, he carefully shaved. Just because the world ended didn't mean he had to be uncivilized. With his house virtually empty and his friends dead, the food he needed would be reduced greatly. In all honesty, he was pissed about Marv and Jerry, but the rest just gave him strange looks when he talked about eating things that humans normally wouldn't. He'd been building up to showing him his game, the rules. The stalk, the hunt, the kill, the feast. It was his religion. He'd been a professional hunter and guide for well over twenty-five years.

It was the last and only thing he'd enjoyed in life. Now his life was in tatters. Dead friends, a daughter who ignored him, and there was the threat of those folks coming back and attacking him. He didn't miss the irony of the situation and had plans to prepare for their eventual arrival. He'd positioned guns in every upstairs room and made sure all the magazines were loaded. He considered setting up traps, but discarded it. He wasn't Arnold Schwarzenegger in the move *Predator*. Tricks and traps…tricks and traps… His mind slipped.

TEARS OF THE WORLD

§ § §

Ken woke up, rubbing his face. The stubble was back, so he must have lost another day. He could only hope Emily had eaten; she hadn't woken him up. He knew it was time for her shot, so he hurried to the bathroom and flushed his waste down with a bucket of water. The water level seemed down, so Emily must have been in here and washed herself up. That made him smile. He got another syringe prepped and a new Band-Aid ready and headed in to give her the injection.

He talked to her softly, lovingly. He smiled when he saw half the food eaten and ran his hands through her hair, told her it was ok if he scared her, that he'd heal up soon. Clumps of her hair came off in his hands, and his mind slipped again.

§ § §

Another morning. He did what he needed to do with Emily. Her indifference was starting to bother Ken, but he promised to go make her favorite. He vaguely remembered hanging a pork belly in the smoke house the day after he got hurt. As long as he had remembered to add fuel yesterday, it should be done by today. His head hurt and his mouth was dry, so he decided to go check on things. He walked out there, marveling at the quiet and solitude of the ranch. Somewhere in the distance a turkey gobbled, a hen squawked, and birds and squirrels made their own song in the branches. The sunlight felt good on his face and he smiled, the scabs on the ruined side tearing open.

The pain didn't bother him, it made him feel alive. Today was going to be a good day. He'd check and see if he could make his daughter's favorite hickory-smoked bacon, and then he was going to work on his plans of revenge. Hit the homesteaders before they hit him. He had a pretty good guess on where they were, vaguely recognizing Blake from town. He was the crazy prepper guy who lived far away from everyone. Didn't even have power or running water, according to the rumors. Knowing who he was, Ken knew who his family was. They had farmed a tract of land that was almost impossible to get to, and when the family died off, Blake was sent to finish his years growing up with a foster family. When he graduated, he'd returned home. Ken hadn't been sure of that when he had tried to question him, but the pain had sharpened his memory since his injury.

That was about the extent of what Ken could remember, but he roughly knew where that old tract of land was, and had hunted near there plenty of times. Ken's wealth and fame over the years had allowed him to open his own ranch, with thousands of acres, but the game was never as much fun unless there was some element of risk. So when hunting alone, Ken would trespass and poach. Just for the sheer thrill.

He opened up the door to the smokehouse and

TEARS OF THE WORLD

lovingly checked the meat. It wasn't ready yet, so he added more apple wood and went back inside to make sure the smoke was coming in good. He smiled and pushed Weston's body, then waved goodbye to Marv, Jerry, and the rest.

"Thanks for hanging around, guys," he joked to himself. His laugh was cut short when the sound of a motor made him pause.

He'd heard that sound off and on more than once since he'd been hurt a couple days ago. Then he stopped, dumbfounded. Had it only been two days? He'd been losing time a lot. Nobody had ever commented on this, but he would just have blank spots in his memory. It'd started when he was younger, but had progressively gotten worse over the years. It wasn't unusual to have two to three episodes per week. Had it been a week? The motor cut off, but a weird combination of acoustics in the hills and the silence of the world made it possible for him to hear it, even if it was over a mile away. It was the closest sound he had heard since Blake and that woman had burned his truck and stolen the other one.

"Rat bastards," he said to no one.

He headed to the garage and got his camo on. He hesitated when it came to the camo paint, knowing it was going to hurt his face and instead went with a boonie hat with mosquito netting. He could still black out the rest of his exposed skin, but his Scent-Lok gear was lightweight and covered all but his hands, which would be in gloves.

"Still, a mile is a mile. Let's go hunt," Ken told

57

nobody again, picking up his favorite weapon.

It wasn't as fancy or flashy as the guns he staged in the upstairs, nor did it hold a lot of shells. He opened the bolt, catching the live round and filling the internal magazine of his Remington 700 chambered in .270. If the engine noise he heard was Blake, he was going to give that prepper hippy a taste of justice for messing him up. He briefly considered telling Emily he was heading out, but his soul was crushed every time she ignored him. Like a coward, he decided to have a talk with her later on. He patted his pockets, finding the railroad map that Patty had on her when he had taken them. Perhaps he'd take a shortcut to Blake's.

"Let's go get some." Ken walked across the small parking lot of the ranch towards a set of groomed trails and then ghosted into the foliage, invisible to the naked eye.

§ § §

Two tics on the radio alerted the squad. The forward observer was alerting them that a target was on the move.

"Lost him." The voice was quiet.

The remainder of the platoon was fuming. They had brought in two more squads to make a full platoon, but they had deserted twenty minutes ago when they learned the real reason they were staking out the hunting lodge. Their muffled trucks firing up had been the loudest thing they'd heard in a long time. They'd been out here a day earlier than even Gerard, their sergeant major guessed. For once, the roads were relatively clear, and they bivouacked in-between long stretches of nothingness.

The only reason the confrontation hadn't turned into a blood bath was that many of the young men who were splitting away from Gerard's held the superior firepower. Their two towed mortars were the first to break formation and head back. Supplies and parts were non-existent, so many of the vehicles were old pickup trucks with mounted heavy machine guns. They looked like technicals from a third-world country, but the two squads of almost twenty people had left with stern faces and their ideals intact.

Gerard hadn't cared much. He'd pretty much gone rogue a month ago and figured it'd catch up with him sooner or later. His three squads versus their two. Nobody wanted to fire on another soldier...so the stalemate happened and they split ways. Nobody died.

"Any movement from the house?" Gerard's muted voice came across the radio clearly.

"Negative, sir."

"Squad one, move in. Squad two, find the man. I don't want a lone wolf sniping us. Squad three, you're lookout. Keep where you are and protect our flank. Move."

No one replied, but the squad tics on the radio were all the acknowledgement that Gerard needed.

§ § §

"Now?" Bobby asked, a fuse in one hand and a lighter in the other.

"No, something's going on," Duncan told him.

"How can you tell?" Corinne asked, lying by the two men.

Duncan pointed to the earwig that he had plugged into the radio.

When one of the rogue guard units had turned tail and drove into their kill zone, they had almost pulled the trigger.

"Are you sure?" Duncan asked what appeared to be no one. "Ok then."

"Stand down, Bobby." He looked at the young man. "Those aren't the bad guys. Not anymore."

"But…"

Duncan tapped his earwig. "Base called, and they are on the horn with someone who has been listening to their encoded conversations. Those guys are the good guys, and they might just be allies."

"I hope you're right," Bobby said and put the lighter down, his hands shaking.

CHAPTER 6

PINHOTI TRAIL, ALABAMA

The dreams of fleeing the suburbs wake Michael. He almost cried out loud, which would have awoken everybody. The cave was warm with their combined body heat. Slowly, Michael stood and tiptoed across the sleeping forms. He went outside to stretch and water a tree. It'd been a long time now since he had lived out here in the wilderness, and he wondered if it was safe for them to go back out. Even if the chief's men were still after them, could they even get to their remote location?

After he was done with his watering, he walked back to the stream that connected to the river and sat down. He hated the dream; he still could see the faces of the men he killed. The lives he saved only offset that guilt a small degree. Someday he'd have to tell Linny and Bret the truth, but not today.

Michael stared into the water, letting his mind go back in time, reliving the day.

John and Michael had ridden to his house on the quad. Michael had packed up everything he thought he might need for roughing it. They had originally planned on going into town first, but when they stopped at Michael's house, he didn't say anything.

"We have to conserve gas," was all John said when he turned off the motor.

He packed several changes of clothes and then went to the garage. He took a lot of gear with him, and still had his big pack frame at the cave, but he didn't want to leave the rest of his fishing gear behind. He'd taken all of the Yo-Yo automatic reels he could, all the spare tackle and spools of line. He then opened the gun safe and took his shotgun, a Remington 870 that he'd used every spring for turkey hunting.

"Better take that too," John pointed to the shelf where his father's 1911 .45 was sitting.

"That's Dad's. He'd be—"

"You need it more than he does right now. He's safe. And damn it, I have to think of Daniel as safe—I have to believe he is better off with the church mission than in this mess. Who knows what danger we're in here. What happened to you today is a perfect example of why…oh wow. What's wrong with that?"

"What?" Michael asked, curious about the

change in John's tone of voice.

"The Impala, is it a sixty-six?"

"Sixty-seven. I've been working on it all year. It's what I got busted in…"

"Big back seat," John said absentmindedly. The man turned bright red when he saw the expression on Michael's face.

"Sorry, Michael. I used to have one of these a long time ago. When my wife was alive, we used to go to the movies in my sixty-six. Didn't mean that to sound—"

"It's ok," Michael said, trying to change the subject.

"We shouldn't leave this here," John told him.

"I don't have the keys. My dad took them because I'm grounded."

"He gave them to me. He was going to let you off early if you didn't get in trouble," John told him, opening the door and sliding in.

The glow of the light surprised Michael, and he jumped when the car fired up.

"I thought all the cars were dead?" Michael asked when the motor was turned off immediately.

"It's too old to have circuit boards. This thing doesn't have anything electronic in it…well, except your new radio. Should have stuck with the stock radio. It was a tube variety." John was grinning.

"Wow, ok. So you want to take the car into town?" Michael asked, feeling hopeful.

"No, that's not a good idea. Let's pack the trailer and push it inside here with your car. We'll come back for it in a little bit."

"Why?" Michael asked, confused but excited that the jalopy he'd been working on all summer still worked.

"Because it might be the only running car around," John said cryptically.

They pushed the trailer inside the garage and closed it back up. After John made sure Michael knew how to use his father's .45, he handed it over to him.

"We go shooting every weekend," Michael told him.

"I thought so, but I wanted to make sure." John had one as well, but he wore it in a holster on his side. Michael tucked his into the small of his back after pocketing two spare magazines.

They had ridden down the streets on the three-wheeler, drawing curious glances from everyone who heard it. They ignored the questions people yelled at them, and within twenty minutes they had made it to the police department. The sound of the quad's motor immediately had the attention of two uniformed officers. They were just standing outside talking and smoking. One of them had stepped inside, and within a moment, the chief stepped out and talked to the man still smoking. The three cops were walking towards the three-wheeler before John turned the motor off.

"Wow," Michael said, worried about how quickly they were being approached. "Do you think they know what I did already?"

TEARS OF THE WORLD

"Nope. I think this might have been a mistake. Keep your shirt tucked in, and if things go sideways, step behind me."

"What are you talking abou—"

"John Norton," the chief interrupted. "How'd you get that thing running? Change the points or something?" the chief asked.

"No, it just works. We're here to report an attempted robbery and—" John was interrupted by the chief as well.

"Well, see here. We're under a national emergency. I'm going to have to confiscate this here piece of equipment. We'll give you a receipt, and when things come back on…" He smiled at them, used to having his own way.

"No, Billy. You aren't taking my three-wheeler. We're here to report an attempted robbery and assault on—"

"Mr. Lewiston, your father told me you'd be out of town this week. I really don't want to have Officer Shepherd and Stark take you in for statutory—"

"I'm not here about your daughter. Sir. Somebody tried to rob me, and he's…"

"Go on," one of the officers said.

"He's dead, sir. His kids are out there and they need—"

"Well now, once we have this quad, we can go take care of it. Step aside," the chief interrupted again.

Michael's temper flared up, but he held his tongue. He stepped behind his friend's father as earlier instructed and waited for things to go south. He didn't have long to wait.

"That isn't going to happen, and quit interrupting me. You guys have nothing working?" John's voice came out between clenched teeth.

"A few old trucks we confiscated last night and this morning. This ride here will be for short distance—"

"You aren't taking my three-wheeler." John took the key out of the ignition and pocketed it, leaving his hand close to his side.

The chief moved one hand that'd been obscured behind one of the men standing beside him to reveal a large black revolver.

"Get ready," John whispered without moving his lips.

The chief began to raise his gun when the other officers started to draw their pistols as well. All eyes were on John, the mild-mannered man they had all known growing up. What they never saw was the man/child hiding behind John pull the .45 from his back waistband. They did see when he took a big step to the side to clear his area of fire, and then it was all gunfire, blood, and noise.

John wasn't a quick draw artist by any means, but he was faster than anybody that Michael had seen on TV. With the police hesitating half a heartbeat, Michael walked rounds into the chief and the man on the right, firing at center mass. John's gun boomed loudly, and he lost sight of him as the horror of the situation dawned on him. Michael quick-

TEARS OF THE WORLD

ly reloaded and looked at the three downed officers. Only one of them was bloody, a shoulder wound. The rest were holding their chests and gasping pained cries.

"Good job. I didn't know if you realized they had vests on," John said, smiling briefly.

"Vests?"

"Oh shit. You boys just got lucky," John said, kicking the guns away from the cops.

"Billy, I told you that you weren't going to take my three-wheeler. It's too soon for martial law to have been called up, so you're doing this bullshit on your own. You're lucky that deputy dog over there just has a crease in his arm."

John continued to harangue them as one by one he ripped their shirts open and unfastened the Velcro on one side of their vests. The chief said nothing, hatred in his eyes as he rubbed his chest in labored breaths.

"You'll go to jail for this. The both of you," he said between pained gasps.

"How about this? I put you in the jail, and in a week, I come back for you three? You just tried to rob a citizen. Hell, you did last night as well."

"We knew what it was," the officer who was grazed said.

"Knew what what was?" Michael asked him, trying to stay out of the way, the pistol forgotten in his hand.

"We got an alert from Homeland Security. Someone tipped them off. We get these about once

67

a week, but when everything died, even the back-ups…"

"Shut up, Shepherd," the chief said.

"We were just trying to get a head start. It was going to happen anyways," the other officer to the right of the chief said.

"Just stop guys, ok? Just stop. Shepherd, let me look at your arm," John said to the man he used to play baseball with as a kid. Shepherd held up his arm, looking at the rip in the fabric.

"Tis only a flesh—"

Michael watched the whole scene unfold before him in a state of shock. When John had his back turned to look at Officer Shepherd's arm, the chief pulled up a pant leg. He pulled out a stubby pistol and aimed it at John's unsuspecting back. Michael's hand moved and shots were fired. The fat, slow .45 slugs tore through the chief's now unprotected chest, and he died almost instantly. Michael stared at all the blood and almost missed the movement to the right of the chief as the officer charged him. Michael got off two quick shots and dropped the pistol as the third man he'd killed that day fell facedown.

"Michael, get your gun." John's voice broke through the haze.

He knelt and picked up the gun, automatically replacing the magazine and pocketing the empty one.

"Shepherd, you know we didn't ask for this," John told him.

"All the same, you are going to have to kill me. You can't gun down a cop, let alone three of us."

TEARS OF THE WORLD

"I'm going to leave you behind. We're going to split for a while. Get that arm looked at. It's mostly a graze, but if you need antibiotics, I'd get it today before everyone goes crazy." He paused to look at the chief before amending, "Everyone else that is."

"You'll be my first priority as soon as—"

"Words, words, words. Those two got what was coming to them. You're lucky. I might let you test your speed against the kid here, but he looks like he's as fast as me. Are you that fast?"

"You have to sleep sometime," Shepherd said, dead serious.

"Yeah, and not around here. In case you can't smell the smoke over the gore, the fire's coming, and it's gonna burn, burn, burn. Let's go, kid," John called to Michael with steel in his voice. Michael backed away slowly so that he didn't turn his back on the downed officer.

Michael was shocked at the sudden shift in Daniel's father. He had always known him as the quiet but helpful dad of his best friend. Inside the man's soul beat the heart of a warrior, and somehow, the beast was back out of the cage.

"What did you do in the navy?" Michael asked as he sat down on the three-wheeler behind John.

"Oh, a little bit of everything. One-man army, remember?"

"You were in the navy," Michael told him, his voice quivering.

"I was a SEAL," John said before firing up the quad and driving away.

BOYD CRAVEN

§ § §

Michael's reverie was interrupted by feet slapping the ground behind him. He turned and smiled as the kids came pouring out of the cave with John bringing up the rear. John saw the pensive look on Michael's face and immediately knew what had awoken the young man from his sleep. The first life he took bothered him, and it continued to haunt his dreams as well. It wasn't as difficult for the ones afterwards, but you always remember your first. Michael had killed three in the space of hours in one fateful day.

"Linny, how are you?" Michael asked as the young girl pounced on him, crushing his ribs in a little girl's version of a bear hug.

"Good. Remember, you're supposed to take us fishing today. Remember?" Bret asked him.

"Oh yeah. Fishing. I don't know if I can stand to go fishing one more time." Michael was teasing, but they didn't know that.

"Oh, come on," Linny said into his chest.

Michael locked eyes with John, who nodded.

"You got it working again?" Michael asked.

"Better than that. I fixed the box that does the encryption. It is pretty crude stuff, but I've got a group in Kentucky I've been following. They're using an open frequency like regular coms, but they probably don't think anyone else is listening," John told him, rubbing each kid on the head before moving on.

TEARS OF THE WORLD

"How do you know where they are?"

"I overheard another conversation," he said cryptically, so Michael dropped the subject. He figured that John needed some time with the radio and hand crank to charge the unit up without little voices to drown out the sound and annoy him.

"You going to check that one out?" Michael asked.

"Yeah. Can't have little ears. It's pretty bad."

Michael nodded and squeezed the kids together, giving them a bear hug.

"Let's go catch some fish," Michael said, giving John a little wave.

"Just not the stinky ones this time," Bret said.

"No, not the stinky ones."

CHAPTER 7

PINHOTI TRAIL, ALABAMA

S o, what's a trout line you're always talking about?" Brett asked as they hiked the trail to the southwestern tip of the lake.

"Yeah, and why is there never any trout, just stinky catfish?" Linny piped up, happy to be out with Michael.

"It's called a 'trotline,' not a trout line, you silly gooses." Michael's mock scolding elicited giggles from the kids. They knew the right word for it, but they wanted to press the old joke.

"What it is, is a heavy line with a bunch of drop lines with swivels and hooks coming off it. The one I have out starts from the riverbank. See this tree here?" Michael paused next to one they had just stopped in front of. On it, a white braided mono-filament line was tied off to the tree with the line

TEARS OF THE WORLD

leading into the water.

"This is where I tied it off. See the first bobber?" he asked them.

"It's a pop bottle." Bret almost sounded disappointed, but his face was scrunched up in a way Michael had come to think of as his heavy-thinking look.

When that kid got that look, you knew he was making money for the bank. He had proven himself more mature and resourceful than many a teenager, let alone any eight-year-old.

"Yes. It'll work to hold the line up where I want it. I have twenty-ounce pop bottles strung out every thirty feet or so."

"Did you have to drink all that pop to make it?" Linny asked, suddenly wishing she had a pop.

"No, I used junk I found floating. Come here, I'll show you a drop line," Michael told the kids, pulling on the line a little.

He was surprised, but there was some heavy tension on the line. The first drop was visible, so he pulled it up and showed them.

"The hook is empty," Bret said, disappointed.

"Yeah, little fish can nibble away at it and sometimes steal the bait, but we'll put more bait on it later on." He dropped the line back into the water.

"So, I can see all the pop bottles going across the lake. Did you have to swim across it to do that?" Linny asked.

"No. I walk the shoreline. I tied the end of the line off on another tree at the other end. Let's hike over there and untie it and pull in the hooks to see what we caught."

"Ok," both kids chorused.

The humidity hadn't hit yet, but the mosquitoes were trying their hardest to make the nominations for the new state bird. They stopped to spray bug repellant and sip from their water jugs before finishing the walk to the other side where the trotline was tied off to the tree. An old dented galvanized metal bucket sat there, with an odd cone shape to it.

"Ok, this bucket was probably forgotten a long time back by folks. Who knows what it was used for, but it's going to help us keep the line from tangling. You ready to see if we caught some fish?"

"Oh yeah," Bret said, jumping in excitement.

"Yes please," was Linny's reply.

Michael smiled. He remembered the first time his grandpa and father showed him this trick. He was never sure on the legality of it, but it caught fish, often times more than enough. It was a good thing too. The Lewiston clan loved their catfish almost as much as they loved spin casting for others. After a month of fish, the kids were starting to complain. All this went through Michael's brain as he untied the line and pulled it in as they walked the shoreline.

The slack line was put in the bottom of the bucket, and when they came to a drop line, the hook was hung from the edge of the bucket. Michael worked in a clockwise motion when he lined up the hooks. Right away Brett picked up on what he was doing, and knew that even though the line in the bucket might be a mess, it was the drop lines that would tangle everything horribly. He finally worked up the courage to ask, and Michael confirmed that was why he was doing it.

Michael silently cursed himself for not explaining everything out loud. Someday, this might be what the kids had to do to survive without him, or without John. Late at night when the kids were asleep, the two men would have frank discussions on what an EMP would do, how the society was supposed to break down according to some study the war college did forever ago. They knew it could happen. They knew that within the first year, over ninety percent of the country would be dead. Suddenly Americans were thrust into pre-industrial America without the knowledge or work ethic our forefathers had. So, forgetting to teach the kids why he put the hooks in the way he did or pulled in the line might be one more tidbit of knowledge lost. He promised himself to be a better teacher.

He was on the twentieth hook when the next one in the line suddenly made the water erupt. A fat catfish splashed as he was dragged from the muddy bottom of the lake.

"Stinky fish!" Linny yelled. But she was excited and jumping up and down while her little brother was smiling so big, his face was almost split in two.

Michael set the bucket down and showed them how to pull the hook out. He held the big catfish by the jaw and found a flat space on the bank. He showed them the spot on its head and then poked it with his fillet knife. The fish spasmed for a bit and then stopped moving. Michael pulled a burlap sack out of his daypack. He handed it to Linny to hold open, and he dumped the dead fish in. She made a face, but the excitement was still there. Michael pointed out that at about the halfway mark, the drop lines were a little longer. Because they were fishing a lake, it was deeper at that point. It was part guesswork, but he was certain it was the deeper lines that held the catfish. In all, they pulled three more fish before they made it back to the other side.

It was just enough food for the four of them for today, barely enough. The greasy fish had been a staple for over a week now since their store-bought food had run out, and they were desperate to find something else. They had talked about sneaking back into town, but were worried about Officer Shepherd and the aftermath of the shooting. They'd even heard broadcasts when they first got the radio going. The National Guard was enforcing martial law. Heavy curfews were in effect, and some guys that John called ham radio guys were talking about FEMA camps.

One guy in particular told them about his experiences. Sure, get on the bus, get some food when you get to the camp. What they hadn't told him was that he had to give up all the food he already had, give up anything that resembled a weapon, including box knives or pocket knives, and that the families were to be split up. Husbands and wives were

TEARS OF THE WORLD

separated by sex, and the kids all dormed together, unless they were over 15. The men worked, the women washed and cooked, and the kids were told to keep quiet. There was never enough food, and to get extra food or some of the MREs, the women and sometimes even the kids would sell themselves to the soldiers for an extra ration. The ham man had escaped with his wife and found his very old radio setup to spread the word.

That was the other reason Michael and John weren't ready to head back yet; none of them wanted to end up in a FEMA camp. Sounded too much like concentration or forced labor camps for them, and so far they had food, just not a lot of variety. Michael showed the kids how to re-bait the hooks from a bag of offal from the night before, and they remade their journey to their starting point from earlier, tying off the trotline again. The pop bottles were in almost the same position, but the wind was blowing the line around.

"Better coverage," Michael joked.

Bret was silent, his face scrunched up deep in thought.

"That's so cool. So you are fishing almost half the lake at once, and you don't even have to be there," Linny said.

"Yeah. Since we're all getting a little sick of cat-fish—"

"Stinky fish!" Bret interjected.

"Ok, since we're all getting a little sick of stinky fish...I put out some lines on YO-YO reels that I hope will catch us some turtles, or even a big pike or something," Michael told them, wishing he had the bouncing energy the ten-year-old girl had.

"What's a YO-YO reel?" Bret asked.

"It's kind of like a trotline, except it reels in when there's any slack. And there's usually only one hook," Michael told him.

"Cool," both kids chorused, which cracked him up.

Michael took them another ten minutes along the shoreline until they stopped. He showed them the silver reel. It looked a lot like a fly reel would, but a little different. Heavy cord tied the device to the tree, and when Michael pulled on the line, it came easily. He showed the kids how if a fish pulled on the line, it'd set the hook and reel the fish in to shallow water. The bait thieves had gotten to this one, so he re-baited the hook and pulled out twenty feet of line. He made sure to hold the end of the line by the sinker and not the hook. He showed them how to do it and gave it an underhanded toss, keeping one hand on the reel in case he threw it too hard, triggering it to retract.

"That's awesome," Linny said, but again, Bret was lost in thought for a moment.

When he didn't move or speak, even his sister stopped to make sure he was ok.

"Earth to Bret, Bret the brat, come in?" she teased, waving her hand in front of his face.

"Bret, you ok?" Michael asked, becoming concerned.

TEARS OF THE WORLD

A change came over Bret's face, and he looked up at them and smiled.

"No, I mean, yes. I'm ok. Michael, do you have more of those YO-YOs?" Bret asked.

"Sure. I brought three boxes of them."

"Can I try something?" Bret asked, his voice pleading.

"Sure. You want the heavy line on one like I'm using for the turtles?" Michael asked.

"Yes, please."

"You are so weird," Linny told her little brother, who promptly ignored her as Michael pulled one out of his daypack and handed it to him.

"I brought spares already rigged up, in case one was broke. I have three more to check. Want to keep going?" Michael asked, watching as Bret's focus turned onto the shiny reel.

"Please," Bret said.

There were no more turtles or fish that day, and their walk back to the camp was happy and upbeat. Before they got to the cave's entrance, Bret stopped them.

"Can I have a swivel and a leader please?" he asked.

"Sure," Michael told him, puzzled at the request.

The line was already baited with a hook, and Bret took off into the brush by the cave. Two weeks ago, they never let the kids out of their sight, but neither of them had gotten lost, and both were becoming quite proficient in finding their way through the woods and home without disturbing the wildlife. Finally, they just told them to stay within yelling distance. It kept the older men sane; neither of them could stand the constant questions forever. Linny reluctantly followed her brother, and Michael headed into the cave.

"Are the kids with you?" John called out from the darkness.

"No," Michael said.

"Ok, come here. What do you think of this?" John asked him, handing him the headphones from the black boxes.

They were part of a radio transceiver set. One was the power supply, the other was the radio itself. John knew it wasn't an old RS-1, but it was the closest thing he could think of. It had a hand crank to recharge or run the unit, and both of them spent over an hour each cranking the first night he put it together to see if the PSU would hold a charge. It had, and now they had a working radio of sorts.

Michael put on the headphones and listened. His face darkened, and he took them off and handed them back to John, who put the headphones on, but left one ear free.

"It sounds like there was a disagreement," Michael said after a moment.

"Yeah, that was my take too. A National Guard unit is defecting. I just can't tell who's who. The Gerard guy sounds like he's going to attack this house, but I have no idea why. For all I know...wait..." a look of concentration came across John's features, and he suddenly hurried to the crank. "No!"

TEARS OF THE WORLD

Anger filtered through his voice as the PSU lost power. "No, no. I was just…"

"I'll crank it, John, you listen," Michael said, gently nudging his friend's father out of the way as he started to crank the handle. After a minute or two, John reached for another box and turned some dials. He smiled.

"Keep cranking Michael," he said, and Michael just nodded.

Michael could hear the kids playing outside now, but they stayed out of the cave. It was a miracle, but after an hour of cranking and two very sore arms on Michael's part, John motioned for him to quit cranking.

"I think I've heard all I need to."

"Good. My arms are cramping," Michael griped.

"Let's go check on the kids," John suggested.

They both walked out into the warm air and sunshine and saw the kids playing with a bag of marbles, a game John had taught them to play. Bret was shooting, and Linny was almost bouncing into the dirt circle they had scraped from the forest floor. Both men looked at the kids, smiling at the fact that they both were happy, probably happier than before the world ended. John's smile faded suddenly, and Michael was certain he was thinking about Daniel, whether or not his son was safe. Michael hoped to God he'd see his best friend again. Not to mention his parents. He missed them something terrible. Michael was about to say something to John when a metallic ping got his attention. Bret was up like a shot and ran to the woods at a dead run, Linny close on his heels. Michael and John ran after them, not knowing what was going on.

"Could that have been a gunshot? Silenced?" Michael panted aloud.

"No," John replied, and they both slowed as they came upon an improbable sight.

Bret was dancing around a rabbit that was suspended over three feet in the air. It had been snared by the wire leader. The YO-YO reel was high up in the air, tied to a tree limb. The rabbit's movements caused the wire to jerk all over the place, so John walked to it and grabbed it by the base of the skull and the hind legs and pulled, severing the rabbit's spinal column before it could choke out. Michael stood in shock and found a rusty beer can that had shot off the line.

"Whoa," John said, pointing at the reel. "Check out what the kid made."

Michael took the improvised snare off the rabbit's throat and pulled the line down to where the loop of wire was at ground level. At first he'd missed the hook, which was now tied at eye level, about two feet below the reel. Bret must have climbed up to set the thing, and he'd also found the beer can to hang on the hook from the pull tab. An improvised dinner bell. Genius.

"Is this how it works?" he asked Bret.

"Yeah. I didn't see it go off, but I did it. I fished for a rabbit and I got one. NO STINKY FISH!" he yelled in triumph, pumping his hands in the air.

TEARS OF THE WORLD

They laughed so hard, there were tears running down their cheeks, and even Linny joined in.

"No, we're still cooking the fish, but I think we're going to have some good eating tonight. Let's go," John told the kids. He turned to point at the snare and then gave Michael a thumbs-up.

Michael shook his head no. He hadn't taught the kid that—it was all Bret!

§ § §

When the kids were fed and asleep, John and Michael talked about the radio conversation he'd overheard. They hadn't had a chance, but what Gerard and his men had planned made their blood run cold. They couldn't understand why somebody from the same area and frequency as the Kentucky group was leading Gerard's men to another group of potential victims.

"A trap! They are leading them into a trap!" Michael said after some thought.

"Sounds about right. That means the group who peeled off today and is calling for central command...start cranking," John said gruffly.

It took John a few tries, but he finally got a response from the Kentucky group. He briefly told them what he knew, how he knew it, and gave them the same information repeatedly. Whoever this David person was, he knew radio gear. But he lacked the same encoding equipment that the guard unit was using. John pleaded with them not to fire on the two squad mortar teams until he could make contact with them. He was told to wait one.

David got some lady on the radio. She sounded young, almost like she had the voice of a pixie. But her bell-like voice had a strength and confidence that had John smiling.

"You ever serve?"

"Two tours, Iraq and Afghanistan. I just retarded. I'm Sandra, by the way."

"What's your last name, ma'am? You sound awful familiar to me now that we've been talking."

"I just got married. I'm Sandra Jackson now."

"I'm John. Ok, let me talk to them boys and I'll get right back to you." John took the headphones off and looked at Michael. "How are we for charge?"

"Good, but I'm cramping. Make it fast."

John made two calls, one long one to the mortar squads who had left Gerard's platoon, and then one to the homestead group, telling them to switch to a different frequency so they could coordinate with the unit.

"Here, I'll take over, boy. I want to listen to the fireworks, and my arms are fresh," John said. Michael gratefully flopped on the ground, shaking his arms out.

"Who was that lady? The one you said you thought you knew?"

"Sounds like her, but if she is who I think she is…" John's words trailed off and he smiled.

"Yeah, is she pretty?"

"She's pretty deadly," he said after a pause. "One

of the finest hand-to-hand trainers the army's ever produced, and one of the best special operators they had. She's almost good enough to be a SEAL," he said with a grin. "I kind of feel sorry for whoever she married. If it's her, she could whoop his ass. Worked with her in Afghanistan about four years ago before I got out of the navy."

"What did she mean when she said she was retarded?"

"Retired. I think she recognized my voice too. That's squid talk. She knew I was in the navy."

"What were you doing in Afghanistan? I thought navy people were all ships and submarines," Michael said, trying to change the subject.

"You know what, for being that dumb, you get a turn at this crank when my arms tire out. This is getting good!" John joked, and they both fell silent. After a while, John pulled one earphone aside and held it away from his ear so Michael could listen in.

Soon, fire and brimstone would rain down upon the wicked. Soon.

CHAPTER 8

Sandra smiled, replacing the handset. Her conversation with Sgt. Smith was surprisingly short, and they both agreed upon a quick change to the battle plan. He asked for one hour to set up, which was quite a lot, considering the raid on the house could be happening at any time. They reluctantly agreed, because they couldn't get eyes too close to what was going to happen. She gave the coms gear back to David, as he was better with it overall, and walked to the table where Blake was sitting with his leg straightened out stiffly in front of him.

"What do you think?" he asked her. "Are they on the up and up?"

"From everything I've heard, yes. They don't know where our guys are, but if they hit Ken's house with the big stuff…"

"While he's inside…" Blake said with a smile.

"Too bad, that. I'm going to make you pay," Ken said, stepping out of the shadows, a wicked knife in his hand.

The knife was pressed to the base of Sandra's throat, and Blake and David froze. Footsteps could be heard running up the stairs. Lisa had been changing to help with potential triage, and she stopped dead in her tracks when she saw her daughter-in-law being held at knifepoint.

"What, who?" Lisa said, knowing almost immediately by the hideous open wounds on the man's face.

§ § §

What remained of Gerard's platoon was pissed. They were communicating on an open channel for ease and letting their boss know he'd been had. They'd tossed the entire compound, and all they found were the corpses in the smokehouse and a half-mummified girl upstairs covered in bandages. They did find a lot of supplies and had started to load them as a consolation prize, but there were no women here. Gerard was losing face and losing his cool in front of his men; he was walking to the communications to get David on the horn when several whistling sounds could be heard. His blood ran cold, and he had just enough time to dive under the deuce and a half, hiding under the engine as the artillery rained down. The shots were spaced apart, but it became apparent that the two squads were using both 105mm howitzers.

The overpressure was too much. Gerard opened his mouth to equalize things when a round hit the truck, just over his hiding place. He never felt himself pulverized into the rich loamy soil of the driveway's shoulder. It was much worse for the men in the compound. The ones not killed outright in the first forty seconds stood in horror, screaming one long note, only to pause to take a breath and scream some more. Some held their hands over their ears, some just curled into a ball, but there was no place to hide from death; it had been let out of its cage.

Squad three, who was left watching the rear of the compound, was spared by the barrage. They tore out of there and down the road, where Bobby and Duncan set off the first set of charges from over a hundred meters away. The timing was almost perfect, and when the steel drum blew two hundred pounds of rock and chain, the civilian trucks were almost obliterated completely. They waited for the smoke to clear, and then radioed the other two guys manning barrels down the road to keep watch, but they were pretty sure they'd gotten them all.

"I think I used too much ANFO," Duncan said to Bobby as half the hillside slid down after the explosion, covering everything with dust and dirt.

Duncan began to direct the cleanup operation, shooting any and all that were left alive. He radioed the all-clear to base, but when they didn't answer, he figured they were on another frequency talking to the mortar unit. Sandra's squad performed flawlessly, and he only wished his daughter were here to see it herself, but she had argued and won the right to oversee operations from the homestead, where she was more useful. She knew what she was doing—she was a top-notch soldier.

§ § §

Ken stood there in shock as he overheard Gerard's men talking about the mummified corpse of the little girl upstairs. Something clicked, and somehow the missing minutes filled his consciousness. Images of him absentmindedly eating a bite or two of her food while he promised her he'd bury her tomorrow. Of wiping down her corpse so the smell wasn't so bad before covering her back up. Of crying for her loss. Missing moments, missing pieces, missing—

The blade cut deep and Kenny fell, his body suddenly numb. David stood there, his hands now empty. He grasped onto a relieved Sandra, almost carrying her to the table.

Kenny could see where he had gone wrong, why he couldn't deal with what was going on. He needed to bury his daughter.

"Is he dead?" Blake asked, pulling his wife's hands away to check her for wounds. There were none.

"He won't be alive for long. You got him in the

spine," Sandra said, walking to the cannibal.

For a moment, she marveled at the man, at his skill. She'd never been snuck up on and outclassed the way he had done so with her, going so far as sneaking into the house unobserved. Past all of their traps. If he wasn't the epitome of evil...

"Please?" Ken coughed. Sandra rolled him to his side so she could see his face better.

"What?"

"Let me bury my daughter."

Lisa had been frozen in shock, but she stormed across the room and picked up Ken's dropped Bowie and plunged it into his heart.

"I want my son back," she told him, holding the knife until his eyes went unfocused and the life left his body.

"Where's Chris?" Blake asked, alarmed.

"I'm hiding under your bed. Is it safe to come out now?" His voice floated out from their bedroom.

"Did you see anything?" Sandra asked.

"I'm sorry, Dad. I hid when the bad man put the knife up to Mom's throat," the boy said, starting to cry, by the sound of it.

"I'm ok, honey," Sandra called, walking to the bedroom as David opened the front door and dragged Ken's corpse out by his armpits.

Lisa was shaking, and she was sobbing. This moment had played out in her head a thousand times already. She expected to feel...something other than relief. In a way, she hated that she just took a life, but she also told herself she needed to get the final blow in, for her son.

"Is he dead, truly dead?" Patty asked, coming from the basement.

Everyone had forgotten about her. In her mourning she barely came up to eat or use the bathroom.

"Yeah, he's toast," Blake told her bluntly.

From the open doorway, she could see David struggle to get him off the porch. He pulled a folded piece of laminated map out of Ken's shirt pocket.

"Hey, that's mine," Patty yelled, running in her bare feet to get the map, the last piece of Neal's inheritance there was, other than memories.

David gave it to her and smiled at the grateful look she gave him. He knew the smallest of things could make people happy, and suddenly everyone was surrounding him and hugging him and patting him on the back. He stood there in shock and turned a full circle.

"You saved me," Sandra said, leaning in and kissing him on the cheek.

He turned forty shades of red and mumbled, "I hope Corinne didn't see that," which made them all bust up laughing. He walked back in and heard the base unit going off. Sgt. Smith was calling. David sat down and listened to the message and turned to Sandra and Blake.

"The sarge can't reach central command. They have to bivouac somewhere and were asking for suggestions." David looked at them hopefully.

Sandra locked eyes with Blake and Blake asked, "So how many people are in a squad?"

"Nine to twelve," Sandra said, smiling.

"Tell them we have food and a warm place to sleep. Have your squad show them in past the traps and have Duncan interview them, unless you want to do that?" Blake said, things coming together quickly.

"We can both handle that. David, make the invitation and let our folks know. Blake, you rest up, and maybe you and Chris should take it easy in the bedroom and let us clean things up in here."

"I love you," Blake said.

"Love you more, silly man. Go play a board game with our son. Shoo."

Blake smiled despite the pain and made his way slowly to the bedroom, where he eventually coaxed a scared Chris out from under the bed. Of all the games he wanted to play, Chris pulled out one of Blake's all-time favorites. Battleship. They played for nearly an hour.

"I-one," Blake said, the old joke still funny to him.

"You sank my submarine," Chris said, crestfallen.

"Wow, really?" he asked.

"Yeah."

"Want to play again?" Blake asked.

"Yes please!" Chris's enthusiasm for a new game overshadowed the loss, and Blake wondered if this was how life was going to be like in this new world.

TEARS OF THE WORLD

Were the tears of the world wiped away by the thought of a new beginning and a new start? He truly hoped so. The smile on Chris's face warmed his heart and gave him hope.

"I-one," Chris asked, smiling wickedly.

"Hit."

—THE END—

To be notified of new releases, please sign up for my mailing list at: http://eepurl.com/bghQb1

ABOUT THE AUTHOR

Boyd Craven III was born and raised in Michigan, an avid outdoors-
man who's always loved to read and write from a young age. When
he isn't working outside on the farm, or chasing a household of kids,
he's sitting in his Lazy Boy, typing away.

http://www.boydcraven.com/
Facebook: https://www.facebook.com/boydcraven3
Email: boyd3@live.com
You can find the rest of Boyd's books on Amazon:
http://www.amazon.com/-/e/B00BANIQLG

Made in the USA
Lexington, KY
27 February 2019